Sun and Rain

Written by Becca Heddle

Collins

The sun can burn.

I need my hat.

It is good to surf.

We sail in a boat.

My feet feel too hot!

The pool will cool them.

Rain turns the soil to mud.

I need boots.

Was that lightning?

I hear thunder. Duck down!

My coat keeps the wet off.

Rain cannot seep in.

Sun

Rain

After reading

Letters and Sounds: Phase 3

Word count: 57

Focus phonemes: /ai/ /ee/ /igh/ /oa/ /oo/ /*oo*/ /ur/ /ow/ /oi/ /ear/ /er/

Common exception words: and, the, I, my, we, to, was

Curriculum links: Understanding the world

Early learning goals: Reading: read and understand simple sentences; use phonic knowledge to decode regular words and read them aloud accurately; read some common irregular words

Developing fluency

- Your child may enjoy hearing you read the book.
- Take turns to read a page. If your child stumbles over a common exception word, such as **we** and **was**, read the sentence again with expression.

Phonic practice

- Focus on the words with long vowels, beginning on pages 4 and 5. Ask your child which word has the /ur/ sound (*surf*) and which has the long /oa/ sound. (*boat*)
- Ask your child to find the two or three letters that make each of these sounds on pages 8–10:
  /ai/ (*rain*) /oi/ (*soil*) /ee/ (*need*) /oo/ (*boots*) /igh/ (*lightning*)

Extending vocabulary

- Read the text on pages 12–13. Point to **seep** and say: I'm not sure what this means. What's good about this coat? (e.g. *rain doesn't get in slowly*)
- Discuss the difference between **seep** and similar words such as: *trickle, dribble, ooze*. Ask: Do you think the author has chosen the best word? Why?